disc

2215

Used Any Numbers Lately?

By Susan Allen and Jane Lindaman
Illustrated by Vicky Enright

Ⓜ Millbrook Press/Minneapolis

For Jack and Anna Marie with love
—SA

For Sandy and Connie—
best friends forever!   —JL

For my brothers, my friends—
Marc, Nicky, and Tony   —VE

Millbrook Press
A division of Lerner Publishing Group, Inc.
241 First Avenue North
Minneapolis, MN 55401 U.S.A.

Website address: www.lernerbooks.com

Library of Congress Cataloging-in-Publication Data
Allen, Susan, 1951–
    Used any numbers lately? / by Susan Allen and Jane
Lindaman ; illustrated by Vicky Enright.
      p.   cm.
    ISBN 978-0-8225-8658-6 (lib. bdg. : alk. paper)
     1. Numeration—Juvenile literature. I. Lindaman, Jane.
II. Enright, Vicky, ill. III. Title.
QA141.3.A49 2008
513—dc22   2007044374

Manufactured in the United States of America
1 2 3 4 5 6 – DP – 13 12 11 10 09 08

Used any numbers lately?

A a

apartment number

Bb

bus # 24

bus number

January 15th

calendar numbers

dollar numbers

E e

HELP! 911

emergency number

F
f

6th floor

HOTEL POOL

floor number

G g

1st grade

grade number

H
h

31

house number

42"

number of inches

J j

8

jersey number

K k

To play
this game,
enter your
password :

hockey 1234

keyboard numbers

license plate numbers

M
m

number of miles

We're number ONE!

Oo

5347

order number

can you come over to play?

phone number

question number

R r

room number

S s

8 chocolate bars
8 peanut bars
12 boxes of candy
6 lollypops
5 miscellaneous
Sum = 39

sum number

T t

5:00 pm

time numbers

U u

Your number's up!

V
v

volume

35

volume number

W w

my dog weighs
110 lbs.

150 lb ON OFF

Vet-Tec
Scale KGS 68

weight number

$X^{x=6-1}$ $x=5$

X

x equals **?** number

Y y

number of years

Z

z

19117

Vicky Kraft
600 Hortter St.
Philadelphia, PA
19117

Poppea Badger
17 Allens Lane
Philadelphia, PA
19117

zip code number

What numbers have you
used lately ?

About the Authors and Artist

Susan Allen and **Jane Lindaman** have been friends for twenty-five years. Together, they have hiked, gardened, ran their first half marathon, and writen three books. **Susan Allen** is an elementary school teacher and librarian in Phoenix, Arizona. **Jane Lindaman** has been an elementary school teacher in Phoenix and in Gilbert, Arizona. She now lives in Springfield, Oregon. Of course, they both continue to read, write, and use numbers.

Vicky Enright has illustrated a number of highly successful Kathy Ross craft titles, including *Crafts for All Seasons*. Enright lives in Andover, Massachusetts, with her husband, two children, and a large brown dog that has a habit of popping up in her books.

Together Allen, Lindaman, and Enright created two companion volumes to this book, *Read Anything Good Lately?* and *Written Anything Good Lately?*